# Dear Primo

## A Letter to My Cousin

Duncan Tonatiuh

Abrams Books for Young Readers, New York

To everyone trying to make a new home away from their home, and special thanks to Julia Gorton for opening this door. —D.T.

The art in this book was hand drawn, then colored and collaged digitally.

Library of Congress Cataloging-in-Publication Data
Tonatiuh, Duncan.
Dear Primo : a letter to my cousin / by Duncan Tonatiuh.
p. cm.
Summary: Two cousins, one in Mexico and one in New York City, write to each other and learn that even though their daily lives differ, at heart the boys are very similar.
ISBN 978-0-8109-3872-4
(1. Cousins—Fiction. 2. City and town life—New York (State)—New York—Fiction.
3. Country life—Mexico—Fiction. 4. Mexican Americans—Fiction. 5. Letters—Fiction.
6. New York (N.Y.)—Fiction. 7. Mexico—Fiction.) I. Title.
PZ7.T66414Le 2009
(E)—dc22
2008046198

Text and illustrations copyright © 2010 Duncan Tonatiuh

Book design by Melissa Arnst

Printed and bound in China
10 9 8 7 6 5 4 3 2 1

Abrams Books for Young Readers are available at special discounts when purchased in quantity for premiums and promotions as well as fundraising or educational use. Special editions can also be created to specification. For details, contact specialmarkets@abramsbooks.com or the address below.

THE ART OF BOOKS SINCE 1949
115 West 18th Street
New York, NY 10011
www.abramsbooks.com

Score! I just got a letter from my *primo*,
my cousin, Carlitos. I live in America,
but he lives in Mexico, where my family
is from. Maybe someday we'll meet!

Dear Primo Charlie,

How are you? Do you wonder like me what life is like far away? I live on a farm surrounded by mountains and trees. My family grows many things, such as *maíz*.

maíz

We have a *burro*, *pollos*, and a *gallo*. Every morning the *gallo* crows and crows.

burro

gallo

pollos

Dear Primo Carlitos,

I live in a city. From my window I can see a bridge and cars zooming by. I can see skyscrapers, too.

Skyscrapers are buildings so tall they tickle the clouds. At night all the lights from the city look like the stars from the sky.

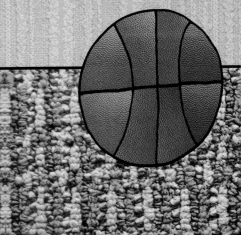

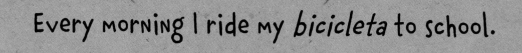

Every morning I ride my *bicicleta* to school.

I ride it past the *perros* and past a *nopal*.

nopal

perros

I ride the subway to school. The subway is like a long metal snake, and it travels through tunnels underground.

At recess time I play *fútbol*. My friend passes me the ball, I kick it with my foot, and if I score, I yell . . . *gol!*

I play basketball. My friend dribbles the ball and passes it to me. I jump and shoot.

The ball goes *swoosh!* Nothing but net.

When I come home from school, I help my mom cook. My favorite meal is *quesadillas*. I make them with cheese and *tortillas*.

After I finish my homework, my mom lets me go outside and play. In Mexico we have many games, like *trompos* and *canicas*.

trompo

canicas

My favorite game is *papalotes*. My friends and I run and run, and with a little wind we fly the *papalote* high up.

papalote

When I finish my homework, I play games with my friends from the building. We play by the stoop . . .

. . . and in each other's apartments, too. I like going over to my friend's home to play video games.

río

In the afternoon it often gets hot. To cool off I jump in a small *río* that is nearby.

In the summer the city gets hot, too. I like getting splashed by the fire hydrant when the firefighters open it up and close off the block.

On the weekend I go with my parents to the *mercado*, an open-air market in the town nearby. We sell *maíz* and *tunas*, a prickly fruit that we grow. We also buy the food and other things we need.

maíz

tunas

On the weekend I go with my mom to the supermarket. She brings a list—milk, toothpaste, soap—and I check off the items as we put them in our cart.

In the town from time to time they
have *fiestas* that last two or three days.
At night there are *cohetes* that light up
the sky and *mariachis* that play and play.

cohetes

mariachis

In my city sometimes we have parades.
People in costumes and uniforms march
down the street, and everyone gathers
around to watch.

There are *charros* in Mexico that I wish you could see. They do tricks with their *caballos* and *reatas*.

charros

reata

caballo

On the streets here you can see break-dancers who do flips and spin on their heads.

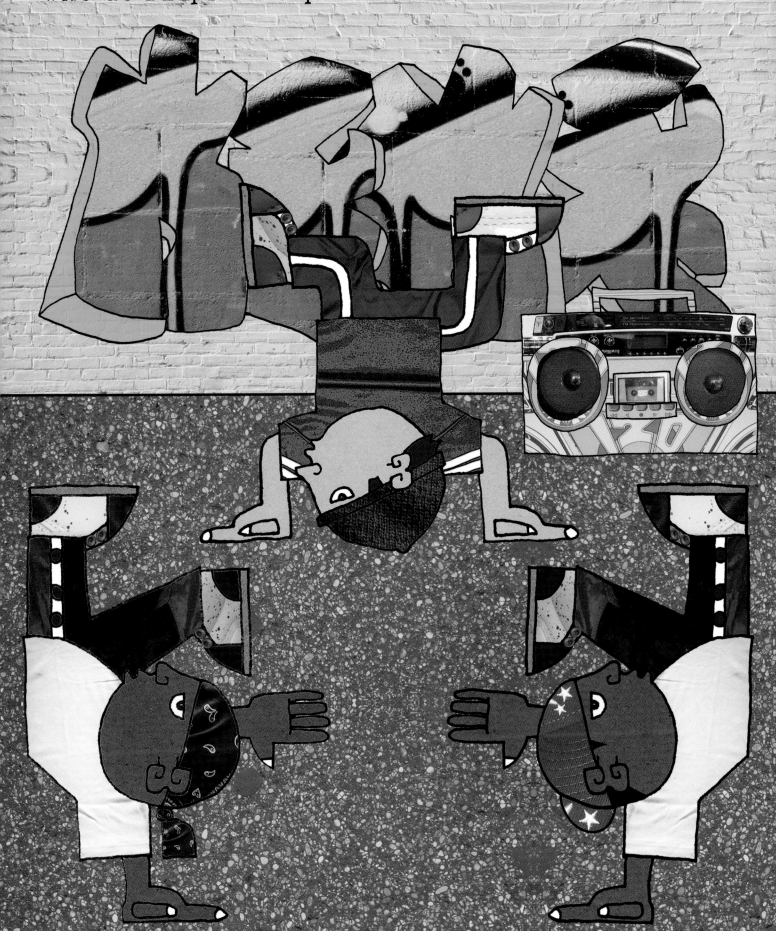

In Mexico we have so many traditions, such as the *Día de los Muertos*, the Day of the Dead.

My favorite tradition is attending the December parties called *Posadas*. At the end of each *Posada* there is a *piñata* filled with fruit and sweets. When someone breaks it, we all get to jump in.

piñata

In America we have traditions, too, such as Thanksgiving, when we eat turkey . . .

. . . and Halloween, when we dress up and go trick-or-treating. But I have to stop writing now. My mom just told me I have to brush my teeth and go to bed.

I have

My primo should come visit me!

# Glossary of Spanish Words

*bicicleta* (bee-cee-**clay**-tah): bicycle

*burro* (**boo**-ro): donkey

*caballos* (kah-**bah**-yos): horses

*canicas* (kah-**nee**-cahs): marbles

*charros* (**chah**-ros): cowboys

*cohetes* (ko-**ay**-tays): fireworks

*Día de los Muertos* (**dee**-ah day los **mwer**-tos): Day of the Dead

*fiestas* (fee-**ess**-tahs): parties

*fútbol* (**fout**-bohl): soccer

*gallo* (**gah**-yo): rooster

*gol* (**gohl**): goal

*maíz* (mah-**ees**): corn

*mariachis* (mah-ree-ah-**chees**): musicians

*mercado* (mehr-**kah**-do): market

*nopal* (no-**pahl**): cactus

*papalotes* (pah-pah-**loh**-tays): kites

*perros* (**pay**-ros): dogs

*piñata* (pee-**nyah**-tah): paper container filled with fruit and sweets

*pollos* (po-yos): chickens

*Posadas* (po-**sah**-dahs): parties given each night from December 16 to 24

*primo* (**pree**-mo): cousin

*quesadillas* (kay-sah-**dee**-yahs): melted cheese sandwiches using tortillas

*reatas* (ray-ah-tahs): lassos

*río* (**ree**-o): river

*tortillas* (tor-tee-yahs): corn pancakes

*trompos* (**tromp**-os): spinning tops

*tunas* (too-**nahs**): prickly fruits, often called prickly pears

# Author's Note

I was born in Mexico City and grew up in San Miguel de Allende*, a small city in the middle of Mexico. My mother is Mexican, and my father is American. They live in San Miguel.

When I turned sixteen, I left Mexico to attend a small, progressive boarding school in Williamstown, Massachusetts, called Buxton. I'd go back to San Miguel during the summer. From that time on, I have been able to experience and be a part of both Mexican and American culture.

Since I was a teenager, I've been aware of the phenomenon of Mexican migration to the United States. A lot of my friends with whom I grew up in my San Miguel neighborhood left before they turned eighteen to work as busboys or construction workers in Texas and other parts of America so that they could send money back to their parents and siblings. I know this is even more true in the rural communities surrounding San Miguel; it's harder to find jobs or make a decent living there.

While in college I was able to see the other side of the migration experience. While attending Parsons I lived in Sunset Park in Brooklyn for a time, where there is a large Mexican enclave. When I first moved there, I was struck by the kids because they looked like me and my friends growing up in Mexico. The big difference was that the kids in Sunset Park spoke perfect "television" English. They wore bubble jackets and Timberland boots to provide warmth from the snow. Traffic lights and concrete were everywhere around them. Back in San Miguel, it was sun, it was T-shirts and sneakers, it was kicking a soccer ball around the cobblestone streets.

I am both Mexican and American (literally; I have two passports), and what I've discovered is that despite the apparent differences between these two countries—the buildings, the food, the day-to-day routines, physical appearances, the politics—at the end of the day, we are more similar than different. People are people.

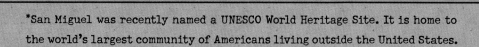

*San Miguel was recently named a UNESCO World Heritage Site. It is home to the world's largest community of Americans living outside the United States.